Shh!
WE HAVE A PLAN
CHRIS HAUGHTON

Peace cannot be kept
by force; it can only be
achieved by understanding.

Albert Einstein

To my youngest sister Lynn

First published 2014 by Walker Books Ltd
87 Vauxhall Walk, London SE11 5HJ

10 9 8 7 6 5 4 3 2 1

© 2014 Chris Haughton

This book has been typeset in SHH

Printed in China

British Library Cataloguing in Publication Data: a catalogue
record for this book is available from the British Library

ISBN 978-1-4063-4232-1 www.walker.co.uk

WALKER BOOKS
AND SUBSIDIARIES
LONDON · BOSTON · SYDNEY · AUCKLAND

MIX
Paper from
responsible sources
FSC® C104723
FSC
www.fsc.org

Shh!
WE HAVE A PLAN
CHRIS HAUGHTON

hello
birdy

shh   SHH!   we have a plan

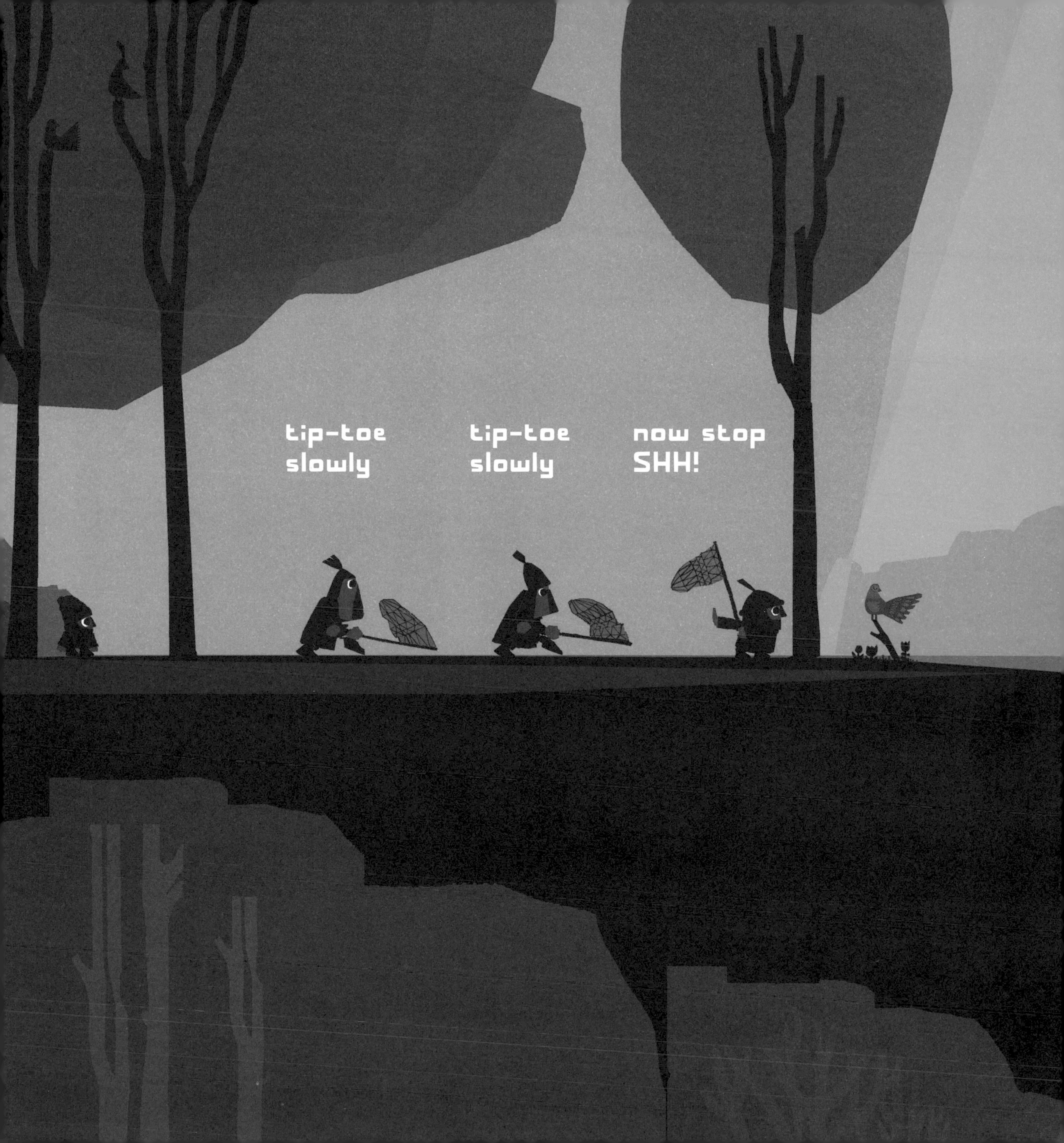

tip-toe
slowly

tip-toe
slowly

now stop
SHH!

ready one

ready two   ready three ...

hello
birdy

shh   SHH!   we have a plan

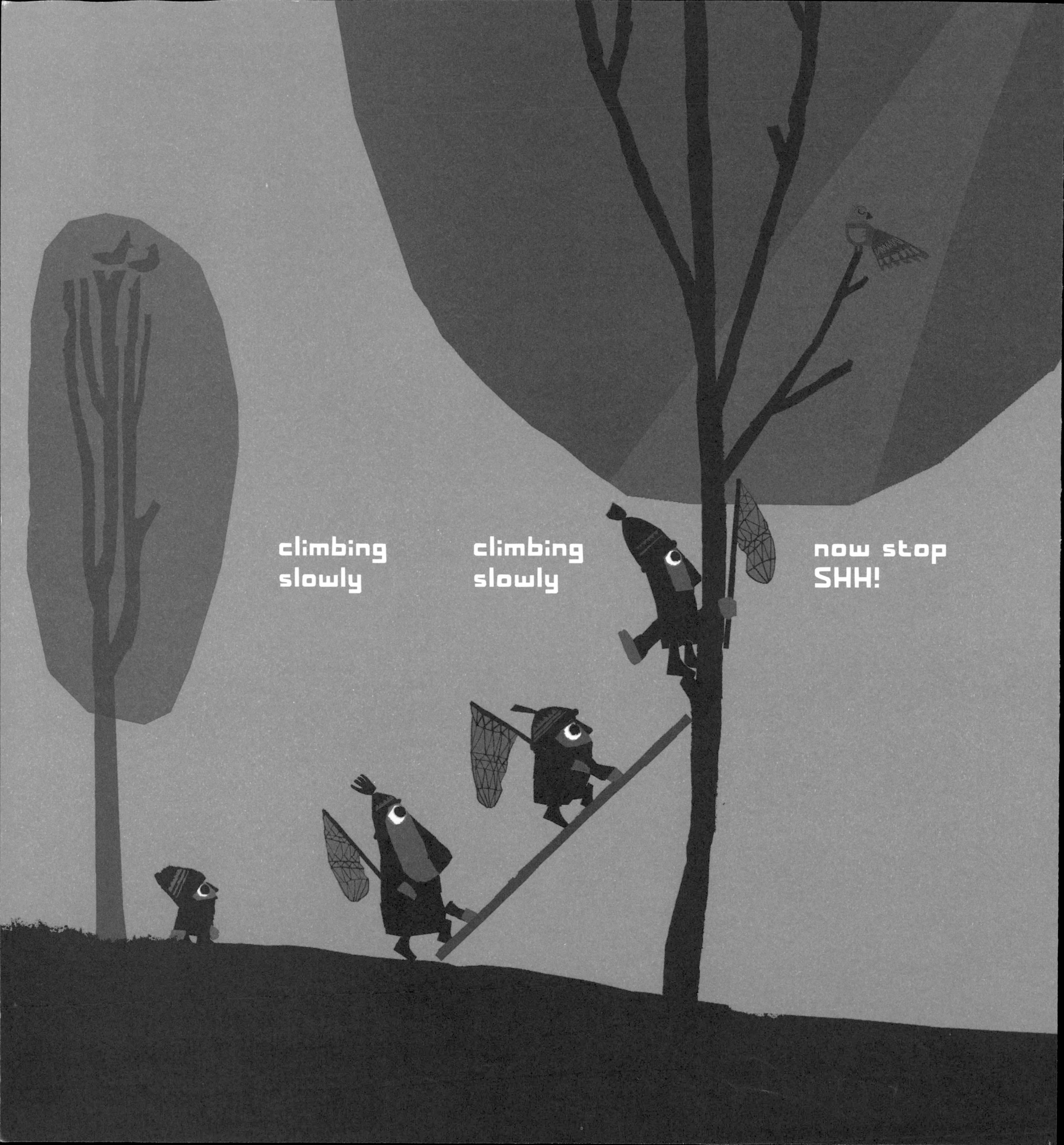

climbing
slowly

climbing
slowly

now stop
SHH!

ready
one

ready
two

ready
three ...

LOOK!
down there

hello
birdy

shh

SHH!

we have a plan

hello birdy

would you like
some bread?

one

two

three

LOOK!

SHH! we have a plan